The Grizzly Revenge

Ruth Brown

Andersen Press · London
Hutchinson of Australia

British Library Cataloguing in Publication Data
Brown, Ruth
    The grizzly revenge.
    I. Title
823′.914[J]   PZ7

    ISBN 0-86264-024-5

First published in Great Britain in 1983 by Andersen Press Ltd.,
19–21 Conway Street, London W.1. Published in Australia by Hutchinson
Group (Australia) Pty. Ltd., Richmond, Victoria 3121.
Phototypeset by Tradespools Ltd., Frome, Somerset.
Printed in Italy by Grafiche AZ, Verona.

In a castle, on a mountain,
Near a lake, and by a fountain,

Lived a Ruler and his lady.
He was cruel and she was crazy.

She kept her servants in a fluster,
Wreaking havoc with her duster.

All day long they'd scrub and clean,
And polish where her feet had been.

She hated grime, that sticks and clings,
But most of all she hated things –

That crept, and things that crawled,
Things that lived in wood or walls.

All day long she raged and screamed,
'Til inside out the castle gleamed.

And then she'd stamp on flies and bugs,
Spiders, worms and snails and slugs.

Even gardeners had their orders,
"Guard all my herbaceous borders."

"If there's a single ant or fly,
I'll want to know the reason why."

Her husband, meanwhile, spent his day
Behaving like a beast of prey.

He hunted all day long and then
At night, he'd go and hunt again.

By day he killed the hare and fowl,
By night he shot at fox and owl.

There was no escape for deer or doe
From the arrows of his bow.

Heads and horns hung round the walls
And ceilings of the castle halls.

In rows and rows of clear glass domes,
Dead creatures stared at polished rooms.

On the floors great skins were spread,
On which the Ruler's feet could tread.

Supple movements, locked in time,
Bore witness to the Ruler's crime.

The Ruler issued a decree
That this year was their Jubilee.

A celebration, for one and all,
Would be held, in the Hall.

When the news spread far and near,
The people all let out a cheer.

For holidays were rare indeed,
In that land of fear and dread.

The Ruler thought for hours and hours
For something special for his spouse.

"She will have a gift so rare
That all who see will stand and stare."

"A crocodile, that's what I need!"
(There were no limits to his greed.)

"A special gift I will provide
From the creature's scaly hide."

Meanwhile, his lady thought and thought
Of precious things to suit her lord.

Suddenly, she had a plan –
A gift, just perfect for her man.

"Go and kill a huge, black bear,"
She whispered in a hunter's ear.

"Bring me the skin and I'll have made
A perfectly stupendous cape."

The great day came and one and all
Were duly gathered in the Hall.

The Ruler said, "My lady fair,
A gift for you – extremely rare."

He gave her, with a loving smile,
A handbag made of crocodile.

His lady murmured, "What a prize,"
And gazed into the glinting eyes.

"And here's a gift for you, my lord,
To warm your back, so strong and broad."

The smile of thanks he gave to her
Showed how much he liked the fur.

"My friends," the Ruler then began
To make his speech of thanks – but then

His lady gave a piercing shriek
Just as her lord began to speak.

Opening her bag and looking in
She found it was no longer skin!

It was very much alive and well,
And lashing out with teeth and tail!

The Ruler saw with great alarm
The massive jaws locked on her arm.

He tried to go to her, but found
His feet being lifted from the ground.

And all the time he felt his cloak
Tightening around his throat.

He couldn't even shout or yell,
His chest was being crushed as well.

No longer was his cloak dead fur;
It was a snarling grizzly bear!

The people watched the gruesome scene,
Unable, first, to move or scream –

Then, as one man, they turned and fled
Through doors and gates and paths that led

As far away as they could get
From that awful scene, and yet –

One young boy took a chance,
And stopped to take a final glance.

Of humans now the Hall was bare;
The couple were no longer there.

He only saw the cold stuffed beasts
Of fur and feather, hair and fleece.

But then he saw one crocodile,
That had a very special smile –

And that big grizzly over there
Somehow didn't seem to stare

In such a very mournful way,
As it had earlier in the day.

No one, since, has ventured near
That castle, looked upon with fear.

Soon it was a tangled mass
Of vines and creepers, weeds and grass,

Inhabited by snails and slugs,
Tigers, bears, and birds and bugs.

For all it was a paradise;
No pain and fear, just peace and life.